DROUGHT

DEREK JORDAN

Brass City Publishing

ISBN: 978-0-9847775-4-9

Published by: Brass City Publishing

340 S Lemon Ave #6271

Walnut, California 91789

Author contact: djordan77@comcast.net

www.jordanmp.com

ACKNOWLEDGMENTS

I dedicate this work to God, family, and friends.

Enjoy!

Derek Jordan

ALSO BY DEREK JORDAN

A Small World

Next of Kin

A Small World 2

A Lonely Married Man (coming soon)

Drought

Drought 2 (coming soon)

Artifacts (poetry book coming soon)

CHAPTER ONE

The streets of Waterbury were deserted. The frigid November weather kept everyone indoors, including the drug dealers. The cold weather wasn't what took the drug dealers off the clock. Election time was in full swing, and every hot spot in Waterbury was frozen. It was the time politicians made promises, and inspired hope among the drug advocates of the Brass City. Law enforcement made their rounds like clockwork. Corner boys suffered, and so did the consumers who kept their pockets thick and healthy. There were, however, a few dealers who predicted a drought and made preparations. If a consumer had those greenbacks, they could afford to spend double on what they normally would spend on an eighth. But there were broke consumers who didn't have that bread, and they were forced to beg for credit from unwilling dealers. Keeping their composure during forced sobriety could be an obstacle.

Tylon Jacobs and Romeo Jackson sat in their cluttered space, mashing the buttons on the XBox One controllers in Tylon's living room. The men stared intensely at the screen while battling in the fourth quarter of NBA 2K21. They were on edge because of the drought that loomed over Waterbury. Some said that the raid in the north end section caused the organized Chas, but Romeo wasn't convinced. He found it hard to believe that not a single dealer had the plant to relieve stress, anxiety, and pain.

The men hadn't smoked in three days, and the tension in their heads was loud and clear. They wanted to keep their own self-inflicted problems as far away as possible. The men were pure stoners. Everyday adversity made them feel hopeless. Tylon lost his job, the mother of his only child, and the majority of his confidence. He felt like he was stuck in a pit of his own shit. His unemployment checks were skimpy after child support, and his baby mother wasn't taking him back anytime soon. Tylon felt down on his luck, and he could use a good puff.

Tylon was tall, brown-skinned, and had a set of teeth with two of them high in his gums. He wore inexpensive clothes, and had a knack for simplifying his life by any means necessary. His apartment was always messy, and he had weed residue all over the place. Tylon was so stressed out that his drive for chasing pussy dwindled since his employer canned him. He used to drive a school bus, but that had come to an end when the bastards in charge surprised him with a piss test. That was three months ago. His rent was past due, and his car was repossessed. The biggest problem he had at the moment was his smoking fixation. The Black and Mild provided him no justice, and the cigar sucked as a replacement for the potent green.

After the game was over, they were struck with silence, steeped in their own misery. Romeo's problems were extensive as well. He came to Tylon's house after sulking all day at his place because of his own fucked up, self-induced bullshit. Romero was a gambler who was in over his head with a huge debt. He created the debt by putting all the money he owned on a horse participating in Preakness. He didn't even like horse racing, but he heard about Rusty, allegedly the fastest horse on the planet. He wanted to scratch the skin off his face when the fine stallion pulled in fourth place.

A domino effect of more bullshit followed after that. Romero constantly had a fucked up attitude towards life because the world threw him a lethal curve ball. He hated everything around him. His Mr. Scrooge personality got darker with each tote of the greenery. Romero's money wasn't consistent, and he worked for a temp agency.

He needed cash, and he wanted it now, but he'd spend his last coin on some weed. The woman he was courting wasn't shit, but he loved her pussy, and he kept her around to fulfill his massive void.

Romeo was a freckled, high-yellow toned man who cracked a six-foot even mark. Although he was stuck with a sorry bitch, and a low wage temporary job, his rap filled voice was remarkable, and he could battle with the best of them. Romero hadn't written any rhymes in a minute because he was on edge, spooky, and in need of any kind of help. Romero had no problem sharing his misery with another defeated soul; the empathy was too great.

After Romeo lost the lead in the game, he hit the big button on the XBox controller and quit. Tylon shook his head, and he wasn't surprised. Romeo always did that shit when the game didn't go his way. Tylon looked at him incredulously.

"That's some bullshit bro. I'm not playing this shit with you no more," Tylon bitched.

Romeo paraded his smirk and pointed at him.

"You tight!!"

"Fuck you," Tylon said.

Romeo laughed some more. "Whatever. The game cheats for you."

Tylon sighed and got up from the sofa.

"I might as well keep the TV on as long as I can. It's a matter of hours before they cut off my cable," Tylon said flatly, ignoring his friend's comment, and focusing again on his own bullshit. Romeo thought about saying something to uplift Tylon's spirit, but fell quiet when he remembered that he had his own bullshit to deal with.

"You speak to Huck?" Romeo asked, changing the subject.

"About an hour ago. Same shit." Tylon sped up his pace and started searching for something. Romeo looked on with curiosity.

"What you looking for?"

"I had two roaches in a sandwich bag, and now I can't find them."

"That's fucked up. Niggas is holdin' out an' shit," Romero snarled.

"If I'm still looking for them, that means I couldn't find them before you came over here asshole. Stop bitching and help me find them," Tylon said.

Romeo gave his friend the finger, but got his ass up and helped him look. After fifteen minutes of creating more clutter, they stopped their search. Romeo beckoned Tylon to pass the Black and Mild he smoked on.

"Somebody somewhere holdin' on to something," Romeo said.

"If cats is selling nothing less than a quarter, we may not have enough for it. Since this drought is thick, prices is going to be fucking ridiculous. And we only have 29 dollars between the both of us."

Romeo scratched his head. "You think your man will give us a loan?"

"In this situation, no."

"We give this nigga business, but he can't look out for niggas?"

Tylon knew Romeo was right. The men gave Huck good business. They put Huck onto the people that dropped serious cash on the ganja every time they dealt with him. Although nothing personal coming from Huck's end, Romeo was using favors and friendships as a card, but Tylon knew it wouldn't work with Huck. He couldn't blame him, but it wasn't like Huck didn't know the men like that. Huck was the only one with weed in the drought, and he charged big time since the drought started.

They grew up in the same neighborhood, and had known each other since childhood. When Huck wasn't dealing, he looked down on the dealers that were too tight to issue a break every now and then. Now Huck was the shit. Tylon was more understanding than Romeo, for Romeo secretly wanted to punch Huck in the face for treating them like the true potheads they were.

Before Tylon had a chance to say something, Romeo beat him to the punch.

"He can't let us go for 29?"

"If he sells his quarters 35 and up, he's probably selling them for 50 since nobody can't find weed to smoke in this drought."

"Fuck that. Call him again. I'll talk to him."

Tylon got comfortable on the couch and channel surfed. He didn't respond to Romeo's request because he knew where that conversation would take them. Romeo and Huck were too strong-minded to have any kind of negotiation. Romero and Huck's pending conversation was a bad idea.

"If you want to talk to the nigga, I can't stop you, but I'm telling you Romeo, the dude ain't accepting no credit right now. We wasting time even thinking about it," Tylon said. He was trying to make Romeo see his point, but Tylon's speech fell on deaf ears. Romeo picked up Tylon's phone off the table and called Huck. Huck picked up on the fourth ring.

"Yo."

"Huck, what up?"

Huck wasn't expecting to hear Romeo's voice and sighed.

"They goin' away for 60. Shit crazy out there and I need this money."

"Can we get a loan until payday?"

"Can't do it bro. I got to move this shit quick."

"Word? You can't do that for us? How about I give you 20 and we'll pay the rest on payday."

"Sorry homie."

"We only got 29 dollars between the both of us. We could pay you back the 31 fam."

"With all due respect Rome, I run a business. If the drought wasn't poppin' off right now, y'all would have that, but right now, this drought is kicking my ass, and I don't have time to wait for money," Huck defended, not realizing his tone escalated a bit.

"Pump your brakes bro. Who you gettin' loud with?"

Tylon bolted out of his stupor, walked to his friend's side, and tried to take the phone from him, but the switch was flipped, and Tylon knew his friend wouldn't stand for that kind of shit.

"Look man, no one is disrespecting you; you called me and you don't like the answer I've given you. Ill tell Tylon the same thing. It ain't nothin' personal. So if you excuse me, I have a business to run." Huck hung up, and Romeo phoned him back instantly.

"Rome, I told you the deal," Huck said into the phone.

"I'm not going to forget this funky shit you're pulling. I'm going to see you," Romeo threatened icily.

"Word? You issuing threats?"

"That's exactly what I'm doing," Romeo said evenly. The phone went quiet.

Huck said, "Just because you got a tag over your head doesn't mean you have to make it my problem."

Romeo blew a gasket.

"Fuck you Huck! I'm coming for you!" Romeo hung up.

"Damn Rome, what the fuck? That's why I told you that we shouldn't bother with him. You know how the nigga is!"

"I didn't like his tone, bro. I accepted the fact that he was being a bitch, but to get loud with me while he's telling me no? I ain't havin' it. I'm going to break his jaw!"

Tylon looked at his friend and shook his head.

"We got to find some smoke man. You going through some ole detox shit. What the fuck did he say for you to lose your cool?"

"The motherfucker said I got a tag over my head. How the fuck did he know anyway?" Romeo looked at Tylon as if he was guilty.

"Fuck is you lookin' at me for? I never whispered a word about that shit," Tylon said truthfully. "You may need to look into that."

Romeo produced a disturbing thought, but he brushed it to the side and focused on the issue at hand. He looked at the trash in Tylon's tight kitchen and couldn't find a roach, clip, or a little weed that might have spilled during its descent into the trash can.

"You talk to Steelz?"

Tylon didn't hear him; he was too busy digging in another pile of clutter looking for those roaches. On cue, Steelz hit up Romeo's phone. Romeo prayed to the gods that Steelz had good news.

"What's good fam? Tell me something good." Romeo placed Steelz on speakerphone.

"I was hoping y'all had the good news. It's still dry on this end. We may have to go OT. Brent told me ain't shit happening no time soon. Popo just did another sweep on Bronson and snatched three or four clown ass niggas and shook 'em down. If another raid pop off, them two niggas is suspect."

Tylon and Romeo didn't want to hear that shit. They wanted Steelz to say that he was on to something, and that he found a connect. They could give two fucks about hungry niggas in the hood.

"Good news Steelz; thanks for sharing that," Tylon said sarcastically.

"Fuck y'all. Y'all motherfuckers don't got good news for me either. What the fuck?"

Steelz had a point.

"You mobile?" Tylon asked.

"That's why I'm calling. I got the whip until tomorrow morning. Bianca doin' a double. "

"Word." The men said in unison.

"So what's the plan?" Romeo asked.

"We'll figure that out when I get over there." Steelz hung up.

"Well, we seeing a little progress," Tylon said while relighting the Black and Mild.

"I hope this dude don't press us for gas," Romeo said.

"You can't squeeze blood from a rock," Tylon said nonchalantly.

The men played another game of NBA 2K until Steelz arrived. Since Steelz had no gas, the men planned their mission from the living room before dipping out to try to cop some decent graded weed. Steelz was willing to add six dollars, the money he was supposed to throw in the tank, making the total of thirty-five between all of them. The men made a few calls and stepped out.

CHAPTER TWO

Huck's pad was drab, messy, and reeked of pussy. His crib had all the signs of a bachelor pad, but the pad was Huck's place, and he took pride in renting his own apartment. The aroma of weed would be pleasurable to the common pothead, and Huck loved for his place to exude the smell of marijuana and incense. In 1929, his great-great-great-grandfather survived the Great Depression by dealing booze. Today, Huck was surviving the drought by being one out of a handful of weed dealers in Waterbury. Weed dealing was simple. When business was booming, he became conservative with money and bought five pounds of piff, stashed the green in case a drought arrived, and kept his business to himself. He believed he could obtain a powerful grip from the five pounds he stashed by placing high drought prices on his product. Huck didn't give a fuck about people's opinions about his high, ridiculous prices, because stoners still paid him big money for his high grade weed. Huck was riding on a high horse.

"Don't even worry about it. Just hit me with that until you get it," Huck said smoothly to the scantily clad hood rat. The brown-skinned chick with a heavy weave hugged him, and sealed the embrace with a peck on Huck's cheek. He watched her plush ass twitch while sashaying down the hallway with a quarter ounce of Blue Dream and credit. After closing the door, Huck adjusted his black silk robe and tied the belt into a loose knot. He relit the clip of Blue Dream, took two large totes, exhaled, and blew a sigh of comfort before placing the medicine stick back into his mouth. With the stick of piff dangling from his lips, he made moves into the bedroom, but stopped in the bathroom on the way there. After busying himself in the mirror, he looked at his reflection, cracked a smile, and knew he was the shit. He was tall, white, and had a set of squinty blue eyes. Huck patted his blond mane to perfection before heading out the door.

When Huck opened the bedroom door, Natalie was laying across the bed with her legs crossed, and the remote control attached to her manicured hand. She was dark-skinned, petite, wore her pitch-black hair short and styled, and had a body out of this world. But she was a whore, and would fuck with anyone she thought had money. Romeo was doing well by her until she found out about his transgressions with his bookies. Everyone had them, but Romeo's issues were deep and life threatening. Natalie was trying to figure out a way to leave their arrangement without hurting his feelings.

She smacked gum while she chewed on it. Huck looked at her and felt a sting of guilt. He'd never thought in a million years that he'd bed Romeo's girl, but he brushed the guilt aside when he thought of Romeo's threat. Huck and Romeo went way back to grade school, but they'd clashed for years over petty shit. As adults, whenever they were in passing or chilling with the same people, they kept it civil, but the underlying animosity was thick.

"You should have given them credit Huck. I know how you feel about Romeo, but Tylon is good people and would pay you," she said convincingly. Her slutty ass was looking sexier with each passing second.

"I hear you Natalie, but come on now, the dude is in over his head. He's hot right now. If I let him go on a loan, I'm literally giving him a gift. Fuck that; I don't trust him right now. If Tylon was solo, yes, I'll give that nigga credit all day, but Romeo...it ain't happening."

Natalie didn't like when Huck used the nigga word, but she dealt with that shit because she was smoking for free in a drought, and she was getting decent white cock. She made a note to playfully check him if he said "nigga" again. She knew Huck's history and that he'd grown up with a hundred percent black population, but a white boy saying nigga still made her a little uneasy, and she never understood why his circle allowed that kind of fuckery.

She put the remote control down and off to the side. She positioned herself on all fours and placed her ass on display. She shook her fat ass like a stripper to entice him. Huck's dick bulged at the sight of her. His guilt went out the window when she pulled her red thong to the side and exposed her clit. She licked her finger, and she slid it into her opening. He took two steps towards her and his phoned chimed. Breaking the mood, he took the phone off the dresser and looked at it. Tylon. If Romeo wasn't looming around, he would have answered, but Romeo was around with anger in his heart. He declined the call and made moves on Natalie. When he mounted her, he ignored the Trojan sitting next to his phone. He tried going for the condom, but Natalie clamped her pussy tight around his dick and fucked him until she felt Huck's nut inside of her.

CHAPTER THREE

Steelz rode slowly through Bishop Street listening to a Maddsonn and Bastard Child collaboration, bopping his head to the supremely lyrical dual. The noise in his head was loud. Women, court cases, and unemployment overwhelmed him; Steelz yearned for a quick outlet.

The high he got from the little weed was wearing off, and he hoped Tylon and Romeo were on to something, but he kept his hope to a minimum. After getting off Burton Street, Steelz rode by Huck's crib and saw Natalie walking out to her car. He shook his head at her, but it wasn't like he never told Romeo how grimy she was. The rumor that she was cheating was floating around, but surprisingly, the affair didn't get back to Romeo. Steelz thought it be best for Romeo to find out on his own.

He pulled over and waited for Natalie to take off. He thought he would pay Huck a surprise visit to see if he could give him a loan. When Natalie's taillights rounded the corner, he got out of the car and walked up to the second floor. He tapped on the door lightly. Huck grumbled and cursed from behind the door before undoing the locks. He thought it was Natalie coming back because she might have forgotten something, but didn't expect to see Steelz. The look on

Huck's face was priceless. Huck closed the door behind him and walked outside to greet Steelz.

"What up?" Huck asked hastily.

"What's good with that green? Can you let me go for a week?" Steelz asked.

"A week? Come on Steelz, you know I can't do that."

Steelz looked at him and nodded.

"Business is business."

'Steelz, you know I would if I could bro. Niggas gettin' mad at me 'cause I can't afford to issue credit. It's a drought man. You right though; business is definitely business and never personal. I'm glad we can agree to that."

Huck wanted Steelz away from him with that credit shit.

"Alright Huck, I know you busy smoking and making money and all that crazy shit, so I'm going to leave you be, but in the meantime, bag me up an eighth of that brain buster shit."

"Steelz man, I..."

"Natalie was sure lookin' good walking down those steps bro. Romeo is a lucky motherfucker."

Huck looked at Steelz and wished he could push him off the porch, but he didn't have the stomach and the heart to do such a thing. It was a pill that Huck had to swallow. Steelz spotted the chink in Huck's armor. and he took advantage.

"Really? You pullin' some blackmail shit Steelz? That's fucked up."

Steelz looked at Huck as if his mind had slipped from his brain.

"What's more fucked up is you fuckin' Natalie behind Rome's back. That's fucked up, and it ain't how gangstas roll."

"Well, I ain't a gangster."

"That's the fuckin' truth. Now go get it."

Huck fumed. He wanted to inflict bodily harm on Steelz, but he knew better. Steelz was half black and Indian; he was small and thin, but the lust he had for guns was bigger than life. Steelz wasn't afraid to use them.

Huck swallowed a huge dose of his pride and retrieved Steelz an eighth. Huck was so pissed he saw red, but he had to roll with the punches. A fight was what he didn't want because it was too much money popping off his gate. He didn't want to draw any heat or unnecessary attention to himself.

"Just don't burn me man. I got bills to pay just like everyone else," Huck said flatly before turning his back and walking back into the comfort of his own apartment, and away from Steelz.

Steelz walked back to the car and pulled out a blunt's worth of weed from the eighth before stashing it. He knew Huck would never see the money owed to him. As far as Steelz was concerned, he didn't feel like Huck should be treated with loyalty; he was a piece of shit.

...

Tylon sulked about his life, and where it was heading. Without his girl and his daughter by his side, he carried around a negative vibe. While Romeo talked shit to Natalie about being inattentive, Tylon paced in the small quarters of his bedroom being heart broken and in need of a blunt. Visuals of men pumping his baby mother's pussy put his mind on a standstill. He wished he could catch them out somewhere and beat the fuck out of them even though he didn't know if Portia was seeing anyone. Tylon thought of the possibility of her seeing someone so much that the thought stayed with him. A whirlwind of negative, dirty, and dangerous thoughts were deeply rooted in his brain. Tylon thought of a different approach. He dialed Portia's number, and let her phone ring continuously until she finally answered.

"What Tylon?" she asked unenthusiastically.

"I just called to say you're a bitch and a whore, and that I hope you die," he said icily.

"Would you like to speak to your daughter? She misses you."

Tylon knew she was trying to be civil, but he could hear the anger in her tone.

"Put her on the phone then bitch," Tylon added for the hell of it. He was so angry with her that he got a kick out of that shit.

"Hi Daddy!" Meadow said excitedly.

"Hey baby! How's Daddy's little girl?" Tylon was guilt ridden because he was faking the funk. He loved his daughter, but he was in the mood to talk shit. Meadow rambled about her day at school, but Tylon was too angry with Portia for him to actively listen to his daughter. She told him some more about her day before giving the phone back to her mother.

"She's doing so good in school Tylon. You should have seen the look on her face when she was presented the student of the month award," Portia said easily.

"Fuck you bitch; just drop her off over my mother's house and disappear," Tylon scoffed before hanging up on her.

He looked at his phone and expected her to respond to his ignorant bullshit, but Portia didn't. Tylon overheard Romeo and Steelz talking that drought shit. He wasn't in any mood to discuss the matter with them, but Tylon couldn't vent alone all night. He was hurting bad on the inside, but his homeboys were tussling with their own web of drama. He pushed Portia and his daughter to the back of his mind, and stepped out his bedroom.

Steelz was finishing rolling a small joint. The sight of the piff erased his anger for Portia. His mouth watered at the sight of the fine greenery. He wondered where the hell Steelz got it.

"Where the fuck did you get this?" Tylon asked.

"Does it matter motherfucker? We smoking some free shit and you questioning this nigga?" Romero hissed.

"This is all we got so it's a deep pull and a pass," Steelz said, ignoring Tylon. Steelz felt guilty for not providing the information Romeo needed to hear, but weed was a number one priority for the moment, and he wasn't in any mood to waste a good night by stopping Romeo from killing Huck. Steelz looked out for his boys for providing some weed, but he was fucked up by using a blackmail to ensure his personal stash.

Despite Steelz's guilt, he was happy to be inhaling the chronic. The men fell silent and replayed their own shit in their heads. The weed brought their anxiety levels down a notch. After receiving the piff stick from Tylon, he stole a glance at Romeo and saw the stress and turmoil on his face. Steelz knew he would have to tell him about Natalie before he found out the hard way.

CHAPTER FOUR

Across town in a swank, low rise house, Sly Bender expertly snapped his fingers, and he beckoned his two flunkie employees to enter his lavish living room. Light-skinned, bearded, tall, and husky, Sly paid his dues during his heyday as a foot soldier in the street, but presently, he had a hand in drugs, prostitution, gun running, and gambling. Smart, witty, and easy going, Sly was a monster to those who weren't in a position to pay him. Romeo ranked high on his shit list, and he intended to do something about it. Mayhem and War would help him do just that. After finalizing his last thought, he flicked the ashes of his Black and Mild cigar and exhaled smoke.

The young thugs in the making looked at Sly with no expression and trace of fear, but they respected Sly's grind, status, and history. They wanted and needed the dough and would do anything to get that fast cash..

"You know where he be at?"

Sly died the Black and Mild out and threw back a shot of Yukon Jack.

"No, but y'all niggas will find him. That yellow motherfucker not paying me my money keeps me up at night. Its time for me to sleep like a baby," Sly said sinisterly.

"And you want me to cut his throat?"

Sly looked Mayhem straight in his eyes.

"You cut that motherfucker anywhere you want, but keep him alive. I need that cash he owe me, and I ain't getting my money from no dead man."

Sly left the two goons in his living room, and he returned from the bedroom with two stacks.

"After you cut him, bring him to me."

"Consider it done bro. With this kind of cake you feedin' us, we'll put a nigga's lights out," War said.

"Whatever motherfucker." Sly opened the door for the two goons to leave. "Don't meet me at no destination empty handed."

The young soldiers said nothing and walked out the house. They didn't like Sly on a personal level, but they appreciated the cash he dished out. Sly was definitely their lifeline.

CHAPTER FIVE

Maddsonn's vocals blared from the warehouse speakers while Steelz drove around town. Romeo replayed the same song three times, but Tylon and Steelz were so high that they didn't notice. Their high was fading fast because of their high tolerance. Steelz cringed at the sight of the gas light; his high faded quickly because he had no money to put gas in his girlfriend's car.

"Fuck!" Steelz scoffed.

"What?" Tylon asked.

"Gas light came on."

Romeo and Tylon remained tight-lipped. They still had twenty-nine dollars between them, and they didn't want to pour none of it in the gas tank. They knew that the weed Steelz brought over came with a price tag.

"Bianca is going to be mad as fuck if I bring this bitch home with an empty tank."

"So what you saying?" Tylon asked flatly, already knowing the answer.

"I need some cash."

Silence.

"We've been riding for hours in this dry ass city lookin' for a lame to let us fly for twenty nine, and now you lookin' to skim our cheddar." Romeo was pissed.

"Niggas wasn't saying that shit when the "L" was burning. Mother-fuckers don't appreciate shit; that's fuckin' niggas for you," Steelz said incredulously.

"Steelz, you know we broke and that we only got twenty nine; not to mention that every dealer is doubling the price for even a twenty dollar sack of bullshit. And you tryin' to lower our pockets. I knew we should have stayed at the crib and called around," Tylon huffed.

"That's some corn ball and bum shit you pulled." Romeo peeled off a five-dollar bill from the twenty-nine between them, balled it up, and tossed it in the front seat. "Corny ass nigga."

"Fuck you Romeo," Steelz said heatedly. "Don't start your bullshit. You smoked, got high, and now you're bitching. I ain't really tryin' to hear that shit right now."

"Chill man. It ain't no need to get aggressive, but Steelz, this is some funky shit you pullin' bro. You knew you didn't have gas on your way over to my crib," Tylon added.

"Y'all some unappreciative ass stoners. I bless y'all with the only weed I got knowing that I could of smoked that shit to the head, but y'all want to bitch. Fuck y'all."

"Fuck you too nigga!" Romeo spat.

"Watch your tone," Steelz warned.

"Who the fuck do you think you talkin' to?" Romeo asked belligerently.

"Both of ya' motherfuckers need to chill the fuck out! We ain't getting nowhere with this shit," Tylon pleaded.

"Who the fuck do you think I'm talking to? Nobody ain't scared of your gambling, bad bet making ass," Steelz shot, ignoring Tylon.

"My girl ain't give *my* pussy away," Romeo countered. Steelz kept his mouth shut and pulled over on Division Street. Even though he was referring to a former fling he still missed, Romeo had a tendency to go for the jugular. Tylon fell silent and looked out the window. He knew Steelz wasn't going to go out quietly. Since the men respected each other not to physically fight, they fought with scornful words. Steelz pulled over quietly and placed a grin on his face.

"How the fuck do a nigga like me come across some piff in this drought? Thanks to your unfaithful bitch fuckin' that white boy, I squeezed a little blackmail so we could all get high," Steelz said maliciously.

Romeo was so shocked that he held his mouth open for several moments until he exploded with anger, swinging his fist from the backseat and connecting with a vicious right that staggered Steelz as he sat in the driver's seat. Steelz turned around and swung, but missed badly. Tylon exerted a burst of energy to separate them once Steelz got a hold of Romeo's arm. Once Tylon separated them, both men panted hard from their explosion. No one said a word. The silence was thick.

"Rome, I told you a long time ago about that chick. She's dirty bro, for real, but Steelz, that's fucked up that you kept that," Tylon said evenly.

"Then don't fuckin' smoke. Niggas been cryin' all day about this drought shit, I bring over the weed, we smoke, now its fuck me," Steelz said, still missing the point. "Rome, I never once told you about that bitch?"

Romeo said nothing. He wanted to hurt Huck.

"Yo, word to everything I owe, I just found out this shit tonight when I seen her walking from his crib. He didn't deny it. I saw an opportunity and I took it. I told him he either give me the shit or I'll tell you. Huck don't want no trouble. I wasn't going to be the bearer of bad news, but I was going to be eventually. No one is selling us shit because we can't even crack thirty dollars. What the fuck?" Steelz said thickly.

Romeo was beyond pissed, but he knew Steelz had a point. Steelz would always be an opportunist despite the deception behind their fix. He knew Steelz was holding out on more smoke, but he decided to leave it alone and focus his anger on Huck and Natalie. After brushing the scuffle aside, Steelz pulled away from the curb and headed to the gas station. Around the corner and a thousand feet behind them, Mayhem and War tailed them in a Toyota Corolla.

Chapter 6-Three days later

. . .

Portia's cell phone rang while she busied herself in the bathroom, but the call was from an unwelcome caller. Tylon has been blowing up her phone for the last two hours, and she was sick of that shit. He was obsessed with her, but an outsider couldn't blame him. She was a light biracial, thick, and green-eyed beauty who could cause car accidents with her presence. She knew that Tylon was reacting out of hurt and anger, but she wasn't hearing that disrespectful shit. Tylon's selfish and insecure ways cut the relationship in two, and he was looking in from the outside.

She ran out of the bathroom wearing only a towel after her phone rang. Without scanning the call, she picked up the phone.

"What Tylon?" she scoffed into her IPhone.

"You better start checkin' your phone before answering it. This is not that stalkin' ass nigga. Open the door bitch," Natalie said playfully. Portia's face remained grim because she didn't think Natalie was funny. She wasn't in any mood for Natalie's scandalous ass. Portia didn't like pop ups and wished she'd call before coming through. Portia hoped she at least had the *choke* since she interrupted a tranquil moment.

After letting Natalie in, Portia went into her bedroom, got dressed, and checked on a sleeping Meadow before joining Natalie in the living room.

"A phone call would have been nice. You don't know what I was doing. I could have been fucking," Portia said sarcastically.

Natalie laughed off her comment. When she fished in her pocketbook and pulled out an ounce of piff, Portia's bitching went right out the window.

"Where did you get this?" Portia knew even the best weed suppliers were out of work for the moment.

"Does it matter?"

"It does. I know for a fact Romeo didn't give it to you."

Natalie looked at Portia and smiled evilly.

"I got it from the white boy. As long as I keep throwing this pussy up in his face, there is more from where this shit comes from."

Portia typically minded her business, but the dirt Natalie was doing behind Romeo's back was cold. Portia felt guilty for possessing the knowledge of Natalie's transgression, but it was none of her business.

"Be careful girl; you don't know how that would play out if Romeo finds out. And the way he is now, there is no telling where his mind is. He's cagey, volatile, and paranoid because of his debt. Him finding out you fuckin' white boy can possibly cost you your life, not to say Romeo would take it that far, but the shit on ID channel is real."

Despite the disrespectful, scornful words that dripped out of Tylon's mouth daily, she still loved him and cared about his wellbeing. Meadow only had one father and she needed him. Association always bred similarity and Tylon could replace a bullet with Romeo's name on it.

"You are playing with fire. They grew up with each other Natalie and things could get real ugly."

Natalie became annoyed and agitated.

"You got a good baby father that helps you with Meadow, but you don't appreciate him. I'm sorry that we all can't get decent men in our lives and spit them out like you do," Natalie said casually as she spread the weed in the opened Dutch Master.

"This ain't about me and Tylon not being compatible; this is about you cheating on Romeo with someone he already has an underlying problem with. They grew up with each other, but they have issues; you fuckin' Huck isn't making the situation better."

Natalie knew Portia was right, but what Natalie decided to do in her life was her business. The women struck a cord with each other and fell silent. Natalie looked at Portia as a friend, and that kind of argument could be a friendship killer. Portia was only looking out for Natalie's best interest.

When Natalie lit the blunt, the women changed the subject. They got high and planned an outing. After the babysitter arrived, the women left the apartment en route to a good time.

CHAPTER SIX

The ramshackle apartment on Irion Street had seen better days, but the place served its purpose. The living room contained two folding chairs, and a worn and dingy green recliner. The safe house had mice, a few garbage bags, a putrid scent, no heat, and three grimy motherfuckers with grand larceny in their hearts. Cake, a local gun runner and Romeo's cousin, sat on the folding chair feeling comfortable in his skin. Cake pumped hard work into the street, but his best and latest hustle was pushing steel. The two cronies in front of him were wild, young, and ready to handle grown up business. War and Mayhem held the weaponry to get a feel for them.

"How much for these two?" Mayhem lifted the sawed off shotgun, held it, and pointed it at the door. He liked it. War wanted the .38 special.

Cake looked at the two youths and wondered why they needed the guns, but Cake's job was to task, not ask.

"Since I got a special going on, I can swing those two for five hundred. Anything lower than that, I'm fucking myself. Take them or put them back in the bag," Cake said brashly.

The goons looked at each other and didn't appreciate Cake rushing them into a decision, but they kept silent. They looked over the guns again before making a decision.

"These shits dirty?" War asked.

Cake screwed his face up at the young fucks. "What the fuck do you think? None of my joints is dirty."

"Yo, you can waste the attitude bro," Mayhem said.

Cake leaned back in his chair and smirked at the youths. He could tell the dudes in front of him were too impatient and inexperienced to participate in any war. Cake was a six-foot-two, bald headed dude with a nappy beard. He felt an urge to show his ass, but business was business; the customer was always right. War and Mayhem looked like brothers; they shared the same average height and caramel complexion. They were decked out in baggy blue jeans, North Face bubble coats, and Timberlands. The scowls on their faces were so deep that one wouldn't think they smiled a day in their lives. They were broke, tired of nickel and diming, and hungry as fuck.

"Will do, but I got business to handle. You niggas could understand that, right?"

Mayhem took one look at Cake and could tell he was no one to fuck around with. Cake said it with the same smirk he greeted the men with when they walked into the safe house. War was about to say something slick, but Mayhem beckoned his crime partner with his eyes to keep his mouth shut.

"Will take them."

War and Mayhem pulled out their wads of money, peeled off two fifty, and handed the five hundred to Cake. They picked themselves and their weapons up from off the couch, gave Cake dap and a brotherly embrace, and bounced. Cake went back to the recliner, sat down, felt a vibrating phone stuck in the crevice of the recliner, and pulled out War's cell phone. He scrolled through his messages and saw something he didn't like. Cake and Romeo had their differences, but he wasn't going to let his cousin go out like that. The motherfuckers planned to inflict bodily harm because of Romeo's debt. Cake was too familiar with Sly and his methods and knew that the next step would involve death. He wasn't having that. Cake placed the Galaxy back where he retrieved it. He knew the young goons would come back for it. Cake wanted to be as cordial and incognito as possible, but War and Mayhem had something coming to their asses. He didn't have a problem with Sly, but blood was always thicker than water.

...

"These niggas is pussy. It ain't no math behind it. All we got to do is run up on the nigga when them two other motherfuckers ain't around. It's easy money fam."

Mayhem heard every word War said, but he was too busy fishing for his phone. He knew he wasn't irresponsible enough to lose his phone in a safe house rented by a gunslinger. War didn't notice his crime partner's confusion until Mayhem placed the.38 on the dashboard.

"What is you doin' man? Put that shit away!" War said thickly.

Mayhem put the gun back into his coat, and continued to fish for his phone.

"What happened?" War asked.

"We got to turn around bro. I left my phone at Cake's spot."

Without uttering a word, War turned around and kept his lips tight. His partner made a fatal error by losing his cell phone. Sly blew both the phones up all day, and there were all kinds of incriminating shit on them.

"Simple shit like this could have our cover blown."

Mayhem thought about saying something in his own defense, but he knew it was a lost cause; he could only hope that Cake didn't pry into his phone.

The crime partners were relieved. Mayhem's cell phone was stuck in the old recliner. Cake claimed he didn't know the phone was lost, but War knew better. He had a feeling Cake planted the phone back where he found it. Cake had better things to do than to hang around a safe house after making a firearm transaction. War made a mental note. After leaving the safe house a second time, War shared his concern with Mayhem, but Mayhem disregarded War's theory. Instead of worrying about Cake's possible intrusion, the men set their sights on Romeo and the money that would come their way once they got a hold of him.

CHAPTER SEVEN

After letting out his homegirl, Huck sat quietly on his love seat and blew out a sigh. The piff he and shorty just smoked had him realizing how fucked up he was for sexing Natalie. He didn't care how Romeo would feel about it if he became hip, but he was uncertain of the consequences. If Romeo were game, he would expect Natalie to suck every dick she set her eyes on, but if Romeo was a sucker for love, he could be deadly.

Either way, Huck's high was getting him nowhere. His OT connect would put a smile to his face though. The two pounds of greenery was created and processed in the sticks of Montana, and the weed was known as brain buster shit. No one on the east coast had it. Huck was riding high, but he felt a rug pulling beneath his feet from around the corner. He pulled out a Beretta and examined it. He wasn't built for bidding, especially for a murder, but he would do it if he had to. As a precaution, the first thing he had to do was stop fucking Natalie, even though the damage was already done. With that in mind, he pulled his *Galaxy* out and dialed a number. Herbert picked up on the other end.

"What's good with those postcards? No delay on those?" Huck asked carefully.

"In motion." Herbert disconnected.

If Herbert left when he was supposed to, Huck figured he should be in New Jersey. Herbert, a red neck from Montana, had to make a run in Virginia, Maryland, New Jersey, and Connecticut. The drop off was supposed to end in New Jersey, but Huck promised him another grand for the extra trip. Paying for convenience saved Huck a risky trip to New Jersey. Besides, if he didn't catch Herbert tonight, Huck would have to wait another month until Herbert made the next east coast run. Overall, it was worth it, and Huck envisioned a cash explosion.

...

Tylon, Romeo, Steelz, and Betty plotted and planned to take Huck's life savings. Betty was a small petite Spanish chick from the Bronx who happened to be in town for a few days. She was Steelz's connect and sometimes lover. She came across Huck's vision in the mall, and Huck followed her. She gave him her attention, and he easily went for and swallowed the bait. They grilled Huck's secret supplier from across the street and couldn't wait until he left Huck's spot. They knew Huck was sitting on cash money since he was inflating the weed prices. Since Huck didn't trust a spot or safe house, he kept all his dirt at home. Now it was time to make a move. Tylon went over the last few details while Romeo provided his two cents.

"I'm still a little wary. Niggas is gettin' eleven year mandatories for them shits."

"He's a drug dealer!" Tylon and Steelz said in unison.

"But still, he's a bitch ass nigga. Bitch ass niggas like to call the cops," Romero said truthfully.

The men understood Romeo's point, but Romeo made a secret vow to have the stick-up go south if Huck decided to act up. Romeo's morale was rail thin, and he was close to being a sociopath. He no longer feared the debt collector. He was looking forward to meeting him. The Glock Romero secretly carried was awaiting its climax.

...

Across town in the Brooklyn side of Waterbury, Portia and Natalie mingled and socialized at a club. The crowd was dense, but the women were having a good time. The music was on point. "S & M" by Rihanna blared loudly. Natalie was high, horny, and ready to jump off with a baller. Portia sipped from her Vodka and orange juice and thought about Tylon. She knew he was going through a bout of depression, struggling to stay on his feet, but he gave everything he could. After all, Portia was unemployed and further down in the dumps than Tylon. She was one more missed payment away from losing her apartment, and the next due date was approaching quickly. She needed Tylon, but she didn't need his bullshit and disrespect. She'd rather take their child and live in a shelter than to tolerate Tylon and his bullshit.

The women sat down and took a break from partying. Portia sat down and looked at the other patrons. Natalie pulled her IPhone from her cleavage and checked her text messages. She thought it would be Romeo harassing her, calling her all kinds of bitches, but to her surprise and delight, she hadn't received one. After Natalie placed the phone back between her tits, Portia knifed her with her elbow and nodded her head in Cake's direction. He was heading toward their table.

"What's up y'all? How's the night going?" Cake asked.

Natalie didn't care too much for Cake, but she kept it civil.

"Good and you?" she asked vaguely. Portia caught wind of the short-changed response.

"How's your son Cake?"

"He's chilling, but peep it, you speak to the infamous trio?"

"Not since earlier, why?" Natalie asked with a subtle attitude. Cake caught Natalie's attitude quick, but didn't want to acknowledge it. There were more pressing things going on.

Ignoring Natalie, he turned his attention to Portia.

"I haven't seen them Cake."

"Have a good night," Cake said before disappearing in the dense crowd.

"Bum criminal ass nigga. Always chasin' pussy. He know damn well he didn't come over here to ask about Rome and company," Natalie spat.

Portia thought differently of Cake's approach. Something seemed out of place. She dialed Tylon's number, but his phone was out of service, which was typical. His phone must have *just* cut off in recent hours because he'd harassed her earlier that afternoon. She dialed

Romeo's number, and the call went straight to voicemail. Portia had a bad feeling, but she couldn't place a finger on it. Without looking too obvious, she left Natalie at the table and searched the club for Cake, but there was no sign of him. Without saying a word to Natalie about her gut feeling, she made up an excuse to leave the club. Natalie was pissed because she wasn't ready to leave, but she honored her friend's request.

After dropping Portia's party pooping ass off, she went right back to the club to continue her mission of finding a lame with cash.

...

Sly stretched his stout body in his Jacuzzi holding a half glass of Hennessey. He reflected on his own brutal lifestyle. He'd come a long way, and from a long line of criminality. He fought hard his entire life for the little he had growing up. He completed several bids, and had it in him to do one more if need be. Sly would die hard for cold cash, and would kill anyone trying to tamper with whatever belonged to him. He was cold, tough, and grimy and took no shit from anyone.

Every time someone owed him money, he got it back promptly. The exception to this rule was Romeo. He didn't really need Romeo's money, but Sly operated solely on principle. If Romeo didn't want a threat of bodily harm or death, he shouldn't have made the bet. He knew nothing of race horsing, and he was a fool to gamble against experience. Besides, Romeo was not his kin, and it was nothing for Sly to lay him down.

After drying off in the bathroom, Sly walked out of it wearing a robe and a smile. He was the shit and he knew it. He walked over to the small bar and poured himself another drink; he pulled out and lit an *Ashton Cabinet* cigar. He exhaled a smoke ring with ease, emphasizing his own smug, comfortable lifestyle. He sighed comfortably. He couldn't believe life was *that* good to him. He felt like the happiest motherfucker in the world.

Sly dug around in his closet upstairs in the master bedroom and came away with a half pound of *Black Widow*. He stared at the weed with contempt. He couldn't believe people were tripping out over that shit, but it kept a lump sum in his pocket. The drought increased his bankroll tenfold because he charged double, sometimes triple if it took

him more than a week to get his hands on a half pound. He thanked
God he never smoked weed. He didn't believe in any drug that would
make his mind lazy, but if he could make money from it, Sly had no
problem making his clientele happy. With ganja in sight and mind, he
placed a call to War. He had to up the ante on Romeo.

"What up?" War asked.

"Prohibition equals opportunity."

War knew what Sly was talking about. He put the phone on
speaker so Mayhem could listen in.

"So what's the catch?" War asked carefully.

Sly grinned. "Romeo."

"We already on that though."

"Tonight. Two hours tops." Sly disconnected the call, leaving the
thugs no opportunity to ask any questions. Even an eighth of greenery
could fatten a dealer's pockets. War and Mayhem knew that. They
knew Sly would provide at least a pound. Greed seeped out of the
pair's mouth as they anticipated a cash explosion. They loaded the
guns they copped from Cake, and they walked out the door to handle
Sly's business.

...

Betty knocked softly on Huck's door. After sending him a tit
picture, Huck invited her over. She heard shuffling noises behind the
door before he answered it. When Huck did, he smiled at her, but the
smile faded when three black masked men rushed into his home. One
of them pistol whipped him to the floor, and kicked him viciously in
the midsection. His body curled and he writhed in pain from the thud-
ding blow. Although the men were masked, Huck knew the faces
behind them. Instead of calling them out, he watched hopelessly as his
former neighborhood comrades swiped everything he had. He knew
he had been selfish with his smoke, but he believed that he didn't
deserve being disrespected, beaten, and robbed. After the masked men
gathered money and product, one of the thugs punched, kicked, and
spat on him some more.

When the men left, he lay in his own blood. Huck had mixed
emotions about losing his come-up, and being beaten up by his former
friends. This went beyond swiping his weed; it was personal too.

Romeo planned it out exactly how it went down. Romeo was the only one doing the fighting. Since Huck squirted semen in Natalie, he was willing to charge it to the game. When Huck thought of his new and only supply being lifted from the trio, he saw red. He thought of vengeance, but the thought went south when he realized he had no one on his side. He had to think of something.

CHAPTER EIGHT

War and Mayhem barged through the front door. They forcefully threw Tylon up against the wall before noticing the divided treasure shining from the kitchen table.

"We hit the jackpot! Don't nobody make any sudden moves! Move and you get bucked!" War threatened. He readied the trigger and aimed it at Tylon.

"Word? Niggas is home invadin' shit?" Steelz recognized one of the assailants.

"Niggas is going to murder shit if you don't shut the fuck up," Mayhem spat coldly and kicked Steelz in his stomach. Steelz folded and clutched his stomach.

After situating Tylon on the floor with the rest of the hostages, War trained the gun on all of them while Mayhem stuffed the money and weed in a duffle bag. Steelz kept his eyes on Mayhem. He knew the kid from somewhere, but he couldn't put a finger on it. And then it hit him.

"Little nigga, I know your mother," Steelz challenged.

Mayhem stopped stashing money and drugs and had a murderous look in his eye. "Watch your mouth."

"Yeah, that's right, your mom is a whore. I busted a nut in her when she was eight months pregnant with you. Cindy is trash." Steelz's tone was cold and provocative. Tylon was sure Mayhem was going to dump his clip into Steelz's body.

Mayhem barreled towards Steelz with a gun in his hand. He inched his face close to Steelz and planted the barrel of the gun against his temple.

"Put the money in the fuckin' bag and lets go!" War roared. He knew Steelz was playing a head game with Mayhem, and it was working. War and Mayhem had been best friends since kindergarten, and War knew for certain that Steelz was telling the truth about his mother. War couldn't blame his crime partner for reacting, but they had an objective, and he wanted to attain it before things got out of hand.

Mayhem slowly backed off. He wanted to shoot the smirk off of Steelz's face.

"Listen to your homie. When I see you, you gon' wish you shot me tonight. Your mother suck a mean dick when she get that crack craving. Ask your boy; he had some of that."

Mayhem ignored him and kept stashing the money and product in the bag. War continued to train his gun at the hostages. The money Tylon, Romeo, and Steelz counted and divided was a powerful grip, and Mayhem wondered whom they stole it from. When Portia walked through the door, their game plan went deep into the south.

...

After Natalie dropped Portia off at her apartment, Portia still had a bad feeling that something was wrong. She had no idea what it was, but the nagging feeling wouldn't go away. She drove around Waterbury aimlessly until she received a phone call from Cake. He told her that he was in front of Steelz's place, and that a robbery was in progress. She arrived at Steelz's apartment in seven minutes.

When she got out of the car, Cake approached her and provided instruction and a revelation. He sold the guns to the two dudes performing the robberies, but he wasn't at liberty to ask questions about whom they were robbing. It was a cardinal rule in his line of business.

"Portia, Ty and 'em is being held captive. Listen carefully."

Portia was shocked and afraid, but she knew her daughter needed her father. She complied.

...

War charged at Portia when she opened the door. He subdued her and placed the last two pieces of rope around her ankles and wrists. After securing her restraint, War got up and saw Cake standing directly behind Mayhem who had his arms raised in submission. The two flunkies had failed to secure the back door. Cake beckoned War to untie his people, and to tie up Mayhem. War was reluctant, but he tied up his crime partner. Cake took back the weapons he sold them, and he untied Portia while Tylon, Romeo, and Steelz went to work on the henchmen. The trio threw an abundant amount of punches, kicks, and objects on them. War fell unconscious, but Romeo wasn't finished. He launched his attack to a different level and continued pummeling War's limp body until Cake pulled him off. Portia saw the helpless men on the floor, and she was worried that she was going to be an accessory to murder.

The men tied, gagged, and duct taped the crime partners before they carried them outside and threw them into the trunk. After collecting the money from the table, Cake jumped in his car while Tylon, Romeo, and Steelz got into theirs and drove off.

CHAPTER NINE

Sly's business meeting was interrupted by a sharp knock on the door. He excused himself to collect money. War just texted him and told him they were on their way, but left out all the specifics. If the crime partners didn't have Romeo or cash on hand, then there was nothing to talk about. After opening the door, he cringed at the sight of War and Mayhem. They were beaten up, and their faces were bloodied. War was barely conscious, but Mayhem seemed to be coming out of his stupor. Mayhem didn't realize he had a duffle bag attached to his hip. They were both sprawled out on Sly's doorsteps. Sly reached for the bag, grabbed it, and counted the stack Romeo left for him. After counting the money, Sly read the note Romeo left in the duffle bag. *Next time, get the money yourself. These niggas is pussy. We should be good now.*

Sly read the note again and chuckled. He couldn't believe Romeo had the balls to come at him like that, but at least he had the money. Now Sly focused on the matter at hand; the guest in his home. He looked at the hired thugs with disgust, and he closed the door on the fuckers.

After sitting back down on his favorite recliner, he looked at Huck and contemplated his proposition. Huck was so fucked up that he could barely walk, and his right eye was swollen and closed shut. Although Sly got his money back, he needed someone in the streets during the drought. He mentally counted greenbacks. All he had to do was avenge Huck's robbery and beat down, and he would have a slave in Huck.

...

Romeo and Natalie had fun at the Poconos. They rode quads, horses, and fucked like rabbits even though she found it odd that he wore a condom on every session. Romeo was relieved that he was no longer in debt, and that he had the Grim Reaper knocking on his door. He did, however, wish he could've skimmed a thousand out of the three thousand he owed Sly, but his life was more important.

It had been two weeks since Huck's downfall from the weed game courtesy of his crew. No one had seen Huck since he was jumped and robbed. Tylon warned them all that Huck's disappearance should be a concern. He also told them that War and Mayhem were lurking around East Farm Street asking questions. At the moment, Romeo wasn't worried about shit. Everything was back to normal. Tylon and Portia rekindled their arrangement and were back in their honeymoon phase, but Steelz lost a court case and had to do an eighteen-month sentence.

Romeo felt good about himself. He kicked his gambling habit, he knew Huck didn't have the heart to come at him, and he was currently high on the exotic weed that he and his friends lifted from Huck.

Natalie held Romeo's knee as he drove the Honda Accord rental on I-80 East. As expected, Natalie had to use the bathroom. Romeo said he would stop at the next gas station. Romeo wore shades, but he stole peripheral glances at Natalie wondering why he was so fucked up over her. Instead of her daily hairstyle of a simple ponytail, her jet-black hair touched the small of her back. Romeo loved when she wore her hair down; it made his dick hard.

When Natalie gave the gas clerk back the key to the bathroom, she walked back to the car. When she lifted the handle to get back into it, the car door was locked. Romeo rolled the passenger window down an inch.

"Romeo, stop playing. It's too cold for this shit. Open the door."

Romeo shot her a grin.

"That wouldn't be a good idea, just like it wasn't a good idea to fuck Huck. I think that's colder than it is outside," Romeo said smoothly while lighting up a roach clip.

Romeo loved the painful look on her face as the frigid air beat at her body. Natalie wore jeans and a North Face jacket, but nothing to cover and protect her hands and her head from the cold weather. She didn't think Romeo knew about her rendezvous with Huck. She couldn't even find the words to defend herself. Romeo's revelation froze her.

"Huck got your tongue," he asked sarcastically.

"We was just cool. Don't look for no confession because there is nothing to confess to. We was cool and we chilled, but we never crossed that line. What the hell Romeo?! We had a great weekend and we made love. Why ruin it over something that is not even there?" Natalie was stunting her ass off and Romeo knew it. "We have a three hour drive ahead of us; please open the door."

Romeo turned the heat up in the car to signal his comfort.

"*I* have a three hour drive. Now get the fuck away from the car."

"No! Open the fuckin' door Romeo! This shit ain't funny! I told you we didn't fuck! What else do you want from me?" Natalie started getting loud and she drew attention from curious eyes.

Romeo smiled. "I don't want nothing from you. This is just a little payback."

Natalie cried and talked shit, but Romeo ignored her as he rolled up the window. She banged forcefully on the car, and she screamed obscenities. Romeo ignored the banging and shit talking, put a Maddsonn CD in the deck, turned it up, and pulled off slowly. Natalie got smaller in his rearview mirror as he took off on the highway en route to Waterbury, Connecticut. Romeo didn't look back, and he didn't think anything of it. The bitch had it coming.

The end.

Made in the USA
Middletown, DE
11 February 2022

60201368R00026